Kry will be *my* best friend, not yours!

"Hey," I say, surprised, as I fling my book bag onto the picnic-table bench.

"Hey yourself," Cynthia Harbison says. "What are you doing here so early?" she asks me, scowling with suspicion. "Waiting for Kry Rodriguez to show up?"

"I'm just waiting for my friend."

Cynthia shakes her head in a pitying way. "Kry is not going to be your friend," Cynthia says, jumping down off the table.

"But you already have two friends," I point out, trying to reason with her as I back away a little. "And I only have one. If I get Kry, though, it'll make us even."

"I don't *want* to be even," Cynthia says, narrowing her eyes. "I want to win! So, tough. It's not gonna happen, Emma."

Other books about Emma

Only Emma

Not-So-Weird Emma

Super Emma

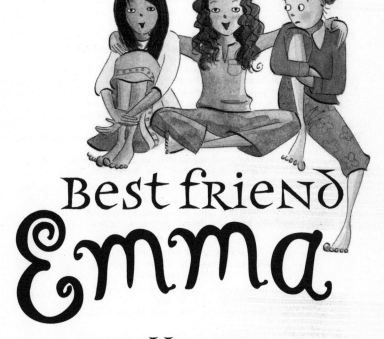

Best friend Emma

saLLy WaRNeR

Illustrated by

jamie HARPeR

PUFFIN BOOKS

PUFFIN BOOKS
Published by the Penguin Group
Penguin Young Readers Group, 345 Hudson Street, New York, New York 10014, U.S.A.
Penguin Group (Canada), 90 Eglinton Avenue East, Suite 700, Toronto,
Ontario, Canada M4P 2Y3 (a division of Pearson Penguin Canada Inc.)
Penguin Books Ltd, 80 Strand, London WC2R 0RL, England
Penguin Ireland, 25 St Stephen's Green, Dublin 2, Ireland (a division of Penguin Books Ltd)
Penguin Group (Australia), 250 Camberwell Road, Camberwell, Victoria 3124, Australia
(a division of Pearson Australia Group Pty Ltd)
Penguin Books India Pvt Ltd, 11 Community Centre,
Panchsheel Park, New Delhi - 110 017, India
Penguin Group (NZ), 67 Apollo Drive, Rosedale, North Shore 0632, New Zealand
(a division of Pearson New Zealand Ltd)
Penguin Books (South Africa) (Pty) Ltd, 24 Sturdee Avenue,
Rosebank, Johannesburg 2196, South Africa

Registered Offices: Penguin Books Ltd, 80 Strand, London WC2R 0RL, England

First published in the United States of America by Viking,
a division of Penguin Young Readers Group, 2007
Published by Puffin Books, a division of Penguin Young Readers Group, 2008

3 5 7 9 10 8 6 4 2

THE LIBRARY OF CONGRESS HAS CATALOGED THE VIKING EDITION AS FOLLOWS:
Warner, Sally.
Best friend Emma / by Sally Warner ; illustrated by Jamie Harper.
p. cm.
Summary: When a new girl joins her third-grade class just before Thanksgiving,
Emma thinks only about gaining her friendship before the popular Cynthia
can, and hurts her best friend Annie Pat's feelings in the process.
ISBN: 978-0-670-06173-0 (hc)
[1. Best friends—Fiction. 2. Friendship—Fiction. 3. Schools—Fiction.
4. Thanksgiving Day—Fiction.] I. Harper, Jamie, ill. II. Title
PZ7.W24644Bes 2007 [E]—dc22 2006027629

Puffin Books ISBN 978-0-14-241217-6

Manufactured in China

Set in Bitstream Carmina
Book design by Nancy Brennan

For little Lucy Parsons, who will meet
her first best friend any day now!—S. W.

X   X   X

For my pal, Al—J. H.

CONTENTS

x 1 x

ᴛHat empty feeLiNG

"I'm stuffed!" I say, almost gasping.

It is a Monday in November, and Annie Pat Masterson and I are eating lunch at school. We are outside, my favorite place in the world to be.

Annie Pat and I are getting ready for Thanksgiving—ten days away, Mom says—by stretching our stomachs. You have to do this from the inside, with food, because outside stretching doesn't work. We already tried that.

"I know you're stuffed. But want another apple anyway?" Annie Pat asks—gloomily, because she is stuffed, too. She holds one out on the flat of her hand, as if I were a horse. Her

A horse can sleep standing up.

red pigtails are usually bouncy, but today they droop.

"Sure," I lie. "We're in training for Thanksgiving, aren't we?"

Annie Pat nods.

"Last year, I was too full after dinner to eat any pumpkin pie," I continue. "And there wasn't any left over the next day, either. So I missed my pumpkin-pie chance for the whole entire year."

"I ate a piece of pie," Annie Pat tells me, remembering. "But I could barely even taste it, my mouth was so worn out from eating turkey."

"It's all that *chewing* with turkey," I say, agreeing with her. "You'd have to be a termite to be able to chew that much."

Annie Pat sighs.

"This is going to be the coolest Thanksgiving ever," I say, trying to cheer her up. "And it's starting early, because on Saturday we get to go to . . ."

"Marine Universe!" Annie Pat chimes in happily. Marine Universe is near San Diego, where the Pacific Ocean is, and it is Annie Pat's favorite treat, because she wants to be a marine biologist when she grows up. I want to be a nature scientist, but I'm not copying her. I have *always* wanted to be that.

Annie Pat's father is taking us to Marine Universe to make up for having a new baby. We have been excited for exactly two and a half weeks.

"It'll be great," I say, as if she needs me to tell her that.

Annie Pat nods, smiling, then pulls a second apple for herself out of a crumpled brown paper bag. Moving shadows from the leaves overhead flicker across her face as her navy-blue eyes stare at the apple. Then she sighs and prepares to take a bite.

She is a very brave kid.

My name is Emma McGraw, and I am the smallest girl in Ms. Sanchez's third-grade class at Oak Glen Primary School, although a boy named EllRay Jakes is even smaller than I am. Annie Pat is the second-smallest girl, after me, and we always eat lunch together—but not because of our size. It's because we're friends.

Also, like I just said, we both want to be scientists when we grow up. Pretty ones, with awesome clothes.

Also, Cynthia Harbison won't let us eat with her anymore.

Cynthia is the bossiest girl in our class, and

the most popular. She always scrapes her chin-length hair back from her forehead with a plastic headband so that it looks perfectly neat, while my curly brown hair goes wherever it wants. And everything Cynthia wears looks new, while I sometimes look as if I got dressed in the dark.

It's not that I'm a slob, but my mind is on other things, my mom always says.

Cynthia also has the loudest voice of any girl in our class. In fact, I can hear her talking right now. She is sitting at a table with some of the other girls in our class. "Fiona is my first-best friend today, and Heather is my second-best friend," Cynthia is saying—mostly to Fiona and Heather. She takes a dainty nip at her sandwich. Its crusts are trimmed off, and it has been cut into triangles. Her mother is very well trained.

"Ooooh!" Fiona says, thrilled. She blushes a little and flips her long, light-brown hair back over her shoulders.

"Oooh," Heather says, sounding like a mourning dove. She looks as though she's about to cry.

That's Cynthia's thing lately—rating her friends. And she sometimes also lists her enemies. But I guess she doesn't feel like it today.

Annie Pat and I swap secret looks. *Relieved* looks.

But even though Cynthia didn't announce this Monday that Annie Pat and I are her first-worst enemy and her second-worst enemy, and even though we have eaten enough lunch for two much bigger kids—or for four normal, us-sized kids—I have that empty feeling inside.

The feeling that comes when you feel left out—like the little lost fish who swims just outside the swooping school of matching fish.

Or left out like the migrating bird who gets separated from its flock somewhere in New Jersey and never gets to visit South America.

Or left out like the smallest, weakest hyena who does not get even a *taste* of the zebra feast. And none of the other hyenas even cares.

I have seen all these things—and worse!—on nature shows, which, in spite of the sad parts, are my favorite things to watch on TV. Annie Pat likes those programs, too.

"Let's go, Emma," she whispers to me, tugging at my sleeve. I can tell that she doesn't want Cynthia, Fiona, or Heather to notice us, because they can be kind of boring, to tell the truth. Especially since they don't want to be our friends anymore.

And school this afternoon is probably going to be boring enough. Why invite even *more* boring into our lives?

"Okay," I whisper back. "We'll throw our trash away and then go run around on the playground."

This is an excellent idea I just had, because it is a cool-hot California day, and the November wind is blowing just the right amount, and my legs feel twitchy inside. They want to *move*.

Also, Cynthia hardly ever runs around on the playground. I guess she's too busy rating her friends.

Annie Pat clutches her stomach. "I'm not so sure about the running-around part," she tells me. "I think I ate too much to run *anywhere*. In fact, I feel kind of funny."

"Then we'll walk," I say, hurrying her along—because Cynthia Harbison's eyes are now sparky, the way they get when she is looking for something to do.

Or someone new to bore.

"Ow, my stomach really *hurts*," Annie Pat says softly as I slam-dunk our lunch sacks into the trash can and high-five myself.

"Come on," I say, dragging her away from the third-grade lunch area. "It can't be that bad, can it? All you ate was—"

"Two tuna-and-pickle sandwiches," Annie Pat says, "and a hard-boiled egg and a sack of oatmeal-raisin cookies and a container of blueberry yogurt and two green apples. And some milk."

And then she moans.

"Well, I ate that much food, too," I point out, "and I'm even littler than you. How come I feel okay?"

"I don't *know-w-w*," Annie Pat says, turning her last word into a howl.

A couple of fifth-grade boys turn to look at us. Annie Pat is bending over now, and she is clutching her stomach even harder than before. "She's gonna hurl," one of the boys tells the other. And then he steps back to enjoy the show.

"She is not," I yell.

Although if Annie Pat *does* throw up, then she'll have that empty feeling, too, I guess. And then we'll match.

"I need to go to the nurse," Annie Pat tells me in a begging voice.

"I'll take you," I say bravely, even though I usually do not like going anywhere near the principal's office.

But my best friend needs me!

10

x 2 x

Who's that?

"We're almost there," I tell Annie Pat, trying to encourage her. "Keep your mouth clamped shut, okay? The way an oyster does!"

Except with an oyster, it's not only its mouth that's kept clamped shut, it's its *everything*.

I guide—okay, *drag*—Annie Pat through the breezeway that leads to where the school offices are. "Mmm," she moans again, in an even more convincing way.

A baby oyster is called a spat.

Lunchtime is almost over, and there are lots of grown-ups buzzing around Oak Glen's front hall—
the way bees buzz around the outside of a hive

when they can't figure out what to do next.

I haven't seen this in person, of course, because I don't have an authentic beekeeper's outfit. Not *yet*.

But the school secretary is talking on her cell phone in the breezeway, where the reception must be good, and the custodian is about to get a drink of water from the drinking fountain, and

the kindergarten teacher is pinning drawings of wobbly people framed in faded construction paper onto a great big bulletin board, and the principal with his big black beard is shaking hands with a mom and her little girl.

Well, she's not really a little girl—she's *my* age. And she's pretty, with a friendly, smiling face, black hair, and perfectly straight bangs that go almost past her eyebrows.

The girl looks at me.

"Who's that?" I whisper, nudging Annie Pat in the ribs.

"Mmm!" Annie Pat reminds me, her eyes wide.

"Oh, yeah," I say. "School nurse. Emergency."

Annie Pat nods three times—fast. If she could open her mouth, she would probably be saying, *"Duh. Hurry!"*

And so I do hurry, because I don't want the poor custodian to have to go get a mop and a bucket of sawdust instead of that nice cold drink of water.

x 3 x

a New Kid in Class!

"Take this late slip to Ms. Sanchez, Emma," the nurse says. "It will excuse you for being tardy. And please tell her that Annie Pat is going home early today with tummy trouble."

Lucky Annie Pat! Even if she does look a little green and groany, lying on her narrow cot. Its plastic covering crackles under the sheet whenever she moves.

Our school nurse wears regular clothes, not a white uniform, and I *guess* she's a real nurse, because she has a stethoscope, squashy shoes, and an official plastic name tag.

But "tummy trouble" doesn't sound like a very scientific diagnosis to me.

I'm not too worried about Annie Pat, though, in spite of the maybe-fake school nurse, because she and I both know the real reason for her stomach ache. But we are too embarrassed to tell the nurse that we were trying to stretch our stomachs. She might talk to us about how half the world is starving.

I know it's true, and I feel really bad about that, and I want to help change things when I grow up. But I am still going to try to enjoy Thanksgiving, complete with pumpkin pie. Is that so wrong?

I sneak Annie

Pat a worried look. *Are you okay?* I try to ask, without using any words.

"Uh-h-h," she says, not even looking at me. She clutches a shiny metal bowl to her chest.

"Scoot, Emma," the nurse says, and so I do.

X   X   X

I wonder what they're doing in class right now?

Probably social studies. Last Friday, Ms. Sanchez handed out photocopied maps of the United States with the states numbered but not named, because the states' names are what we're supposed to be learning lately.

And you can't just make up any name, either, even though the kids in my class came up with some pretty good ones. For instance, Jared Matthews said that Florida should be called "Gun State," because it looks like a pistol that is pointing at the rest of the country.

EllRay Jakes said that Wyoming should be

called "North Rectangle" and Colorado should be called "South Rectangle."

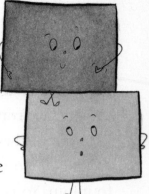

Cynthia said that Idaho should be called "Leprechaun State," because according to her, it looks like a sitting-down leprechaun.

And Annie Pat said that Rhode Island should be called "Teensy-Weensy State," which I think is the best made-up name of all. But people don't get to vote on what the states—even their own state—should be called. If I got to choose what to call our state, California, I'd name it "Bendy State," because it bends in the middle. (You have to look at it on a map to get what I mean.)

Being all alone in the school halls during regular class time is fun and scary at the same time. Fun, because you can do anything you want. You can zigzag from wall to wall instead of trying to keep out of the way of bigger kids. You can spend as long as you want at the sweaty-cold drinking fountain. You can stare at the framed photographs of all the principals Oak Glen Primary School has ever had and imagine them with red wax lips or twirly mustaches.

You can even take the time to go to the bathroom in peace, instead of trying to hurry *and* not make any embarrassing bathroom noises, which is an impossible combination to pull off in a small, echoey room full of girls.

Going to the bathroom at Oak Glen Primary School is my least favorite thing.

Being alone in the halls is also scary, though, because a grown-up could appear at any second and demand to know why you aren't in class.

Even when you have a good excuse, you can't help feeling guilty.

I don't think it's fair that grown-ups are so big and kids are so small.

But the fear of running into a grown-up is enough to make me hurry—a little—to class.

"*There* you are," Ms. Sanchez says as I slowly push open the rear classroom door. To my surprise, that friendly-looking girl Annie Pat and I just saw in the breezeway is standing in front of the class next to Ms. Sanchez.

A new kid in class! And right before Thanksgiving, too. That's unusual.

The new girl is pretty, like I said before. She is tall and thin, and her shiny black hair falls over her shoulders like water. She is completely not nervous, which is completely unlike *me* on my first day at Oak Glen—only nine weeks ago.

To my surprise, she smiles at me and gives me a little wave, like she knows me!

"Where's Annie Pat, Emma?" Ms. Sanchez asks as I hand her the late slip.

"She had to go home early," I announce, feeling important. Especially in front of the new girl.

Cynthia turns her head away from Ms. Sanchez, puts a finger on her tongue, and does an imitation of someone throwing up.

How does she know? There is no point in even asking, because Cynthia seems to know everything that goes on at Oak Glen. That is the source of her secret powers.

Everyone who sees Cynthia do this laughs, and the new girl laughs, too, but not in a mean way. After all, she doesn't even know Annie Pat. Not yet.

"Please take your seat, Emma," Ms. Sanchez tells me, coaxing a few stray hairs back into her bun with her engagement-ring hand. "We were just getting to know the newest member of our class, Krysten Rodriguez. Also called 'Cry,'" Ms. Sanchez adds, confusingly.

She gestures to the board behind her, where she has written the new girl's name in perfect cursive—but with a star over the *i* in "Rodriguez." Just for fun, I guess. And then Ms. Sanchez spelled out *K-R-Y* underneath the longer name.

"That's her nickname," Cynthia calls out, which you are not supposed to do in our class, but Ms. Sanchez lets it pass this time.

And then Cynthia flashes a big kiss-up smile in the new girl's direction.

I can already tell that Cynthia is trying to claim Kry for her own.

We'll see about that! Because Cynthia already has a first-best friend and a second-best friend, and neither one of them is me or Annie Pat, even though we try to be nice to her.

Cynthia and I used to be *kind-of* friends when I first started going to Oak Glen, but now I only have one friend, Annie Pat Masterson. So it makes sense that Krysten Rodriguez, the new kid in class, should be mine.

Mine and Annie Pat's, I mean.

After all, we saw her first!

4

Round One

I called Annie Pat at home last night, but her mom said she was already asleep and she couldn't come to the phone. So I have had to come up with a plan to get Kry Rodriguez to be our friend all by myself.

There are other girls in my class besides the ones I've talked about so far, of course, but they already have each other, so I haven't gotten to know them very well since I changed schools last September. Three of the other girls are best friends from church, and two are next-door neighbors. They always hang out together.

The main girls I have met in my class at Oak

Glen are the ones I've already named: Cynthia, Heather, Fiona, and Annie Pat. And this morning, before school starts, I am going to meet Kry.

Like I said before, I actually used to be friends with Cynthia Harbison when I first started going to school at Oak Glen. In fact, I really hoped for a couple of weeks that Cynthia would be my new best friend, but something happened.

Don't ask me what, though, because I couldn't really tell you! Cynthia just turned against me one day, and that was that. Maybe she got bored once I wasn't new anymore. But by then I had Annie Pat, so who cares?

I used to go to Magdalena School for Girls. It was private, and I never lost any friends there—until I had to leave, that is. But my mom got fired from her regular job, which was being a librarian for a big company near San Diego, and we had to move twenty miles from our house into an Oak Glen condominium. She works at home now.

I almost never see my old friends anymore, and when I do it's not the same.

I am not crazy about living in a condo, if you want to know the truth. There are no pets allowed, which is just terrible for a girl like me who loves nature. Also, my mom and I suddenly have a whole lot of instant neighbors who live very close by, and their cooking smells weird.

Not like ours.

Also, you can hear scraps of other people's conversations, TV shows, singing, and sometimes even fighting, even when you are just walking around outside minding your own business. Even when you put your hands over your ears and sing, "La, la, la!"

You're supposed to be perfectly quiet, though. Especially if you're a kid.

"Bye," I murmur to my mom on Tuesday morning, and I tiptoe out the front door, hoping to get to school very, very early. This is the first part

of my plan to make friends
with Kry before Cynthia gets
a chance to.

So far, it's the *only* part of my
plan.

"Do you have everything?" Mom
calls after me, forgetting to keep her
voice down.

I nod and make a circle with my fingers
to show that everything is okay, and then I
head off down the street.

It is cool and foggy outside today, with
the kind of drizzle falling that feels more
like tiny prickles on your face than it
does like rain. The droopy eucalyptus
trees' crescent-moon leaves rustle and
sigh as I walk down Candelaria Road.

"Br-r-r," I whisper to myself. But really, I am
prepared for this drizzly day. I am wearing a cozy
pink sweater that is nearly new. It is the color of
bubble gum and is soft, fluffy, and reminds me of a

little pink lamb, and my pants flare out perfectly, just like Kry's did yesterday.

She will think I look cool. Cool enough to make friends with today, that's for sure.

I can't wait to get to Oak Glen, which is four blocks away. Even though I miss Magdalena, Oak Glen Primary School hasn't been so bad. That is, if you ignore the boys, which I mostly do—except for Jared Matthews, who can be kind of mean, so you have to watch out for him. And except for Corey Robinson, who sits next to me in class, and smells like chlorine because he swims so much, and is afraid of arithmetic. He's nice. And except for EllRay Jakes, who is the smallest—and loudest— kid in the third grade. I like him, too, though. He's funny.

X X X

"Hey," I say, surprised, as I fling my book bag onto the picnic-table bench where most of the third-graders gather before school.

"Hey yourself," Cynthia Harbison says, because she is sitting there all alone in the foggy gloom— right *on* the picnic table, so she can have a good view of who's coming, I guess. "What are you do-ing here so early?" she asks me, scowling with sus-picion. "Waiting for Kry Rodriguez to show up?"

"Maybe. Maybe not," I say, shrugging. "Why do you care, anyway? Unless you're waiting for her, too. Is that why you got here so early?"

Cynthia is usually the last person to get to school. It's part of what makes her famous.

Cynthia shrugs, not answering either of my questions. She takes off her headband, flips her short straight hair forward and then back in a businesslike way, and then scrapes her headband over it so hard that little comb-stripes show in the hair just above her forehead. She looks as if she is ready for *anything*.

"Don't answer me, then," I say with a shrug of my own. "Because I don't even care. I'm just waiting for my friend."

"Barfy Pat Masterson?" Cynthia jeers at me. "Who probably won't even be in school today?"

"Annie Pat never actually threw up," I remind her.

Cynthia shakes her head in a pitying way. "Kry Rodriguez isn't going to want to hang out with girls who smell like you-know-what. Or with you, either."

"Why are you being so mean to me?" I ask her. "Ms. Sanchez says all us girls should try to be friends. She says she's tired of all the squabbling."

"Ms. Sanchez can't make us like each other," Cynthia says, her chin in the air. "Not once we're on the playground. Kids are the boss of that. *I'm* the boss of that, and I decided I don't like you."

"But—I still like *you*, Cynthia," I tell her, telling the almost-truth. "We used to have fun, didn't we?"

"We had fun *once*," Cynthia snaps. "Because I felt sorry for you when you were new. But now it's over, so give it up, Emma."

"*You* give it up," I say, wishing suddenly that I could push Cynthia off the table. I don't want to hurt her or anything—I would just like to see her go flying through the air like a wicked witch.

"I can't give it up," Cynthia tells me, smiling a little. "Because Kry is going to be my new best friend. I just have a feeling." And then she shivers in a fakey *I-can-tell-the-future* kind of way.

"Maybe not," I tell her, trying hard to keep my voice steady. "Maybe she's going to be *my* new best friend." I seem to have forgotten about An-nie Pat, I realize after a second. But that's okay, because so far, she's not here today.

"Kry is not going to be your friend," Cynthia says, jumping down off the table.

What's Cynthia going to do, sock me? I don't *think* so.

"But you already have two friends," I point out, trying to reason with her as I back away a little. "And I only have one. If I get Kry, though, it'll make us even."

"I don't *want* to be even," Cynthia says, narrowing her eyes. "I want to win! So, tough. It's not gonna happen, Emma."

"Tough, *back*," I echo, not backing up anymore.

I didn't want to fight with *anyone*, even Cynthia.

But it looks like round one of our fight for

My Big Chance

Kry Rodriguez is already in class when Cynthia and I finally go inside. Kry is sitting in her newly assigned seat near Jared Matthews, Stanley Washington, one of the girl church-friends, and one of the girl neighbor-friends. I don't get to sit near Kry, but at least Cynthia doesn't, either.

Annie Pat isn't here today. I hope her stomach didn't pop.

I also hope that she's okay by Saturday, Marine Universe day.

"Let's sit up straight and pay attention on this cold, wet Tuesday, ladies and gentlemen," our beautiful teacher Ms. Sanchez says after she has taken roll. "We're going to review how to write a book report this morning, because I want your finished reports handed in before Thanksgiving. And then, after recess, you'll take turns subtracting multidigit numbers at the board."

Next to me, Corey Robinson groans. I'm not sure which is worse for him: multidigit subtraction or having to stand at the board in front of everyone. But put the two things together, and Corey would rather be swimming in a small tank with sharks. And not the fun kind of sharks, either.

Some sharks can grow a new set of teeth in a week.

"Now, what are my two main rules for doing book reports?" Ms. Sanchez asks, perching on the corner of her desk. She looks extra pretty today. She is wearing a rose-and-cream flowered dress and shoes with tiny high heels and narrow bows on the front. I'll bet she's going out on a date with her fiancé after school is over! His name is Mr. Timberlake, but he's not the one on MTV. Ms. Sanchez's Mr. Timberlake works in a sporting-goods store.

You should see her engagement ring.

Hey, that's something I could talk to Kry Rodriguez about! Because Ms. Sanchez is the prettiest teacher at Oak Glen, and the girls in my class *love* talking about the details of her life—even though we don't know very many of them. But that doesn't slow us down.

I could be the one to bring Kry up to speed about the stuff we *do* know, however. She'll be so grateful! She'll *definitely* want to be my—

"Emma?" Ms. Sanchez is saying. She gives me a scowl.

I blink. "Yes?"

"What is my first rule about book reports?" she asks a little too patiently—as if it is not the first time in the last minute that she's asked me this question.

"We have to read the book. The *whole* book," I add hastily. Because Ms. Sanchez does not believe in skimming. For instance, you can't read *Sarah, Plain and Tall* and then just say it's about a plain lady who is also tall.

"That is correct," Ms. Sanchez says with a sharp, satisfied nod of her head. "And EllRay, can you stop bothering your neighbor long enough to tell the class my second book-report rule?"

EllRay—who has been making upside-down faces at Heather—stares up at the ceiling, thinking hard. His jaw sags open a little. It is so quiet in class for a moment that you can hear the big wall clock tick. *Ka-chuck, ka-chuck.*

"EllRay? Are you still with us?" Ms. Sanchez asks.

"Oh! Oh!" Heather says, raising one arm high and leaning over her desk.

Ms. Sanchez barely hides her sigh, because Heather *always* thinks she has the answer to a question—even when she doesn't have a clue. "Yes, Heather?" Ms. Sanchez says.

"The second rule is that we have to end the report right," Heather says, triumphant. "We can't just say, *'To find out what happens next, you'll have to read the book!'*"

Ms. Sanchez looks pleasantly surprised. "That is correct, Heather," she says, smiling. "Good girl. Now, let's move on to book-report headings. Who knows what information to put at the top of your report?"

X X X

During morning recess, which comes between language arts and math, Kry has to stay inside with Ms. Sanchez and fill out some forms. So no one can try to make friends with her.

The sun finally comes out—right after recess, naturally, but that raises my hopes.

And when the lunch bell rings, Ms. Sanchez asks *Cynthia* to stay behind for a few minutes so she can go over a subtraction problem with her. Score! It's my big chance to make an impression on Kry Rodriguez without Cynthia being there to bother me. But how can I do it?

I could tell Kry a joke, but I can never remember jokes when I need them.

I could say how nice she looks today, which she does, but after she says, "Thanks," then what?

I could give her half my sandwich, but she might not like my current favorite, peanut butter and crunchy lettuce on a bagel. Not everyone does.

For instance, Annie Pat's favorite sandwich is tuna and sliced dill pickles on pumpernickel bread. *Urk.*

Annie Pat's probably not eating that particular sandwich today, not if she still has "tummy trouble."

"Hi," Kry says to me—to *me*!—when I get near the table where the third-grade girls usually eat She is sitting at one end of the table, while Fiona and Heather sit at the opposite end of the table, silent. The other girls in our class are probably eating in the cafeteria today.

Fiona and Heather probably don't even *want* Cynthia to make friends with the new girl, because where would that leave them? Or maybe they are just feeling shy—the way I am. And we aren't even the ones who are new.

Kry peeks up at me through her long, straight bangs, and she smiles, waiting.

"Uh, hi?" I murmur, turning my reply into a soft, wimpy question.

"How's your friend?" Kry asks, looking concerned. "The red-haired girl who—who didn't feel good yesterday?" she adds, stumbling a little as she tries not to say "throw up," "puke," or "hurl."

Kry Rodriguez has very good manners! Now I *really* want her to be my friend.

Besides, it will drive Cynthia crazy if she loses this battle, and then she and I will *really* be even. Because—why did she turn against me for no reason?

Even though I have Annie Pat, it still hurts.

"Who? Annie Pat?" I ask, as if I have lots of sick friends Kry might be asking about, though I think she might be referring to this particular one. "Oh, she'll be fine," I say, instantly dismissing whatever is wrong with Annie Pat.

(Sorry, Annie Pat.)

"That's good," Kry says, and then she pats the bench next to her. "Want to sit here?" she asks, smiling at me again.

Do I? This is going better than I could ever have planned!

"Sure. I guess," I say, shrugging in what I hope is a casual way—because I want Kry to keep on thinking that being friends with me is *her* idea. That'll really drive Cynthia nuts! "I—"

"Sorry! *Taken*," a high, shrill voice rings out, and Cynthia Harbison flings herself onto the picnic bench—right where Kry just patted.

My seat!

And then Cynthia flashes me a triumphant smile.

x 6 x

Round two?

It is Thursday, exactly a week before Thanksgiving. I have stopped trying to stretch my stomach, though, because now I have much bigger problems than making room for pumpkin pie.

Namely, my battle to make Kry Rodriguez my new best friend.

Mine and Annie Pat's, I mean.

Kry is being nice to Cynthia, Fiona, and Heather, but that doesn't mean much, because she's being nice to everyone—even to the church-friends and the neighbor-friends, who probably don't even notice—and to *me*.

Kry is an equal-opportunity smiler.

It's almost as if she doesn't *care* who her new best friends are. And that just doesn't make any sense! At least not to me. I like to keep track of things like that.

Thank goodness Annie Pat is back in school today, because that means this will be a fairer fight for Kry's friendship. Annie Pat looks perfectly fine, not green and groany at all anymore.

She could have come back to school yesterday, Annie Pat tells me, only her mom wanted to be extra careful. (Whenever I get sick, my mom can't *wait* for me to go back to school! But maybe that's because she works at home. Annie Pat's mom doesn't have a money job right now because like I said, she just had a new baby. It's a boy named Murphy. He has red hair, too. I guess it runs in the family.)

I called Annie Pat every night to see how she was, and to fill her in on our battle for Kry.

To tell the truth, Annie Pat doesn't seem that into it!

But maybe now that she's back in school, Annie Pat will see how important it is for Cynthia not always to get her own way. It's *crucial*.

The meanies shouldn't get to win *all* the time.

"How did you ever get the nickname 'Kry'?" Annie Pat asks Kry Rodriguez shyly a few minutes before school starts. The mornings have turned nicer, and a bunch of us girls are clustered around one of the third-grade picnic tables. We are curled over the top of it like shrimps in a shrimp cocktail. Yum.

"I think Kry is a *cute* name, Annie Pat," Cynthia says, as if Annie Pat has just insulted Kry by asking the question. Cynthia scowls in her almost-friend's defense.

"Me, too," Fiona and Heather chime in—though more to please Cynthia than to flatter Kry, in my opinion.

"Who said it wasn't?" I ask, defending Annie Pat.

Kry laughs. "I got my nickname from my

two big brothers 'cause I was supposedly such a crybaby when I was little," she says, answering Annie Pat's question. "*Wah, wah, wah.* Every little thing! Like if the dog wouldn't let me dress him up in doll clothes, or if I didn't get the first pancake on Saturday morning, or if I couldn't find one of my Barbies."

"That's just darling, Kry," Cynthia says, beaming in a possessive way.

"Yeah," Fiona and Heather echo weakly.

More kissing-up—from all three of them. It's really revolting.

"How did you get *your* nickname?" Kry asks Annie Pat. She's not just being polite, either. She sounds as if she really wants to know.

And even *I* have never asked Annie Pat this important question! That makes me feel kind of bad.

Annie Pat blushes, which is a very easy thing to do when you have red hair. "My real name is Anna Patrice Masterson," she tells Kry—and the rest of us. "Those were my grandmothers' names, Anna and Patrice."

"They *sound* like grandma names," Cynthia mutters very softly, and Annie Pat blushes some more. But Kry won't hold what Cynthia said against us, I reassure myself, because I don't think she even heard.

"Shut up," I tell Cynthia anyway—because she can't insult my best friend that way.

Cynthia draws back, all fake-innocent and everything. "*I* didn't say anything," she protests, holding her hands up in the air.

What a liar!

But Kry is looking at me a little nervously, as if she's not sure what to expect next from such a hot-head.

"*You* shut up, Emma," Heather says to me. Her long hair is pulled back so tight into its high-up ponytail that she can probably barely blink. Heather sneaks a wide-eyed glance at Cynthia to see if she notices how loyal she is being.

"Yeah," Fiona croaks. "Stop being so mean, *Emma*."

Me? Mean?

"See, Emma's always starting fights," Cynthia pretend-explains to Kry. "But we try to be nice to her, because I guess she can't help it. Her parents are *divorced*," she whispers, pulling Kry gently

away from the picnic table just a few seconds before the bell rings.

Kry gasps, and she shrinks away from Cynthia's hand.

She's horrified about the divorce, I guess.

And for some reason, I can barely catch my breath. In fact, I feel as though I am about to start crying. I never knew that being a divorced kid was so bad!

Maybe *this* was why Cynthia didn't want to be friends with me anymore.

"Come on, Emma," Annie Pat says softly. "We'd better get going. Class is about to start, and we don't want Ms. Sanchez yelling at us."

I stumble along next to Annie Pat, thinking, *So what if my parents are divorced?*

Why is Cynthia using this against me?

And I also think about the battle for Kry Ro-driguez.

Was this the end of round two?

I didn't even know it had started!

7

a fight with the Wrong Person

This is all Annie Pat's fault, I tell myself later in the morning as Corey Robinson staggers zombie-like to the board for some more double-digit subtraction. If Annie Pat's real name wasn't so dumb and—and *grandma*-like, this never would have happened.

And it's my mom's fault, too—for getting divorced! I never knew it would rub off on me this way. But now that Kry knows all about my messy family, she will *never* want to be my friend.

Unless I think of something fast.

x x x

"Hey, Kry," I say, sprinting over to where she is sitting one second after the lunch bell—buzzer, really—rings. Or buzzes. "Can you come over to my house on Saturday? Because my mom wants to treat us to lunch at a really fabulous place and then take us to a really cool movie. We can even drive over and pick you up at your house."

This will be news to my mother, but once I explain what happened this morning, she'll go along with it. I hope.

Kry blinks, surprised. She has very pretty eyes the color of acorns, and flappy black eyelashes that look like long, delicate, caterpillar legs. "Saturday? Sure," she says, breaking into a wide smile. "Okay. What time? And do you know where I live?"

"You can tell me later," I say, because Annie Pat—*Anna Patrice*—is tugging at my sleeve. I try to shake her away for a second so I can finish talking to Kry.

I hope Cynthia is watching this!

"What?" I finally say to Annie Pat, whirling around, because she just won't leave me alone. But it's okay, because Kry has just waved goodbye and has gone to get her lunch.

"What do you mean, 'What'?" Annie Pat asks me. Her face is pink, and she looks really mad. At me.

At *me*! What did *I* do? I shrug to show Annie Pat how confused I am.

"You—you asked that new girl over on Saturday," Annie Pat says, tears gathering in her navy-blue eyes.

"So what?" I say. "You can come, too. I was going to invite you, in fact," I add, fibbing a little.

I mean, I probably would have thought of inviting Annie Pat eventually, only I hadn't exactly gotten around to it yet.

But Mom is going to freak, being suddenly asked to take three girls to two expensive places in one day. She probably thought we would just take a nice long inexpensive walk that day, and then maybe do the laundry or something.

And usually that's fine with me, because we both love peace and quiet.

"You were already gonna spend Saturday with *me*," Annie Pat says, her tears spilling over.

"Huh?"

"Marine Universe," Annie Pat says, hissing the words like a beaked sea snake, her favorite venomous creature.

Oh, no. "I forgot all about it," I say, the words barely making it past my suddenly dry lips.

"You *forgot*?" she says, almost squealing. "But you said you really wanted to go. And we were gonna do some *research*. Marine Universe is my favorite thing in the whole wild world!"

(Annie Pat says things such as "whole *wild* world" instead of "whole *wide* world." It's one of the things I really like about her.)

"And we were going to treat you to the whole thing," Annie Pat continues. "And we've been planning it for, like—like, six whole months!"

"Two and a half weeks," I say, correcting her. Because I didn't even know Annie Pat six months ago. Six months ago, I was minding my own business at Magdalena School for Girls, which is many miles away. For all I knew then, Oak Glen didn't even exist.

"Shut *up*," Annie Pat says, clapping her hands over her ears.

"No, listen," I say urgently. I try to pull one of her hands away so that she will hear me, but she's pretty strong for the second-littlest girl in the third grade. "Listen, Annie Pat," I repeat. "We could ask *Kry Rodriguez* to go with us to Marine Universe.

That would *really* impress her. It would be awesome!"

And Cynthia could never compete with that, I congratulate myself silently. Again, score!

"I don't *want* to impress her," Annie Pat says, stomping her foot. "Who cares about Kry Rodriguez? She's not even a scientist like us. She'd just ruin the whole thing."

Whatever happened to my battle with Cynthia Harbison? I am suddenly having a fight with the wrong person.

"Kry wouldn't ruin it," I say, trying to convince Annie Pat to see things my way. "And she'd be so happy to be invited that she'd *want* to be my friend. *Our* friend, I mean. Because I'm doing this for you, Annie Pat," I add, desperate.

This is not exactly the truth, but it could be.

I mean, Annie Pat doesn't know it's a lie. So maybe she'll go for it.

But Annie Pat stomps her foot one more time, which is never a good sign with her. "You were our *guest*," she reminds me angrily. "And a guest doesn't get to invite other people along. Especially not for the whole day—and when it's such an expensive treat."

Oh. I never thought of it like that. I guess she kind of has a point. "But—but what can I do,

Some kinds of penguins can jump almost six feet in the air.

Annie Pat?" I ask, holding my hands out in a helpless way. "I already invited Kry to do something on Saturday! And I can't back out now. I can't just un-invite her, can I?"

"Don't even worry about it, Emma," Annie Pat says,

suddenly as cool as an emperor penguin—in spite of the tear tracks on her cheeks. "You and what's-her-name can do whatever you want, because I take back my whole invitation to you. So there!"

And then she turns around and leaves.

8

Round three

It's not fair that Annie Pat is so mad at me. I didn't mean for anything this bad to happen! I just sort of forgot about Marine Universe on Saturday, that's all. Isn't a person allowed to forget something every so often? Am I supposed to be *perfect*?

And anyway, I was trying to make friends with Kry Rodriguez for *us*—me and Annie Pat—so we'd be even with Cynthia, Fiona, and Heather.

Annie Pat didn't even look at me the whole rest of the day. But I am willing to forgive her for that, so why can't she forgive *me*?

And now, on top of all my other problems, I have to convince my mom—who worries about spending too much money when we use up toilet paper too fast—to take Kry Rodriguez and me out on Saturday for a fabulous lunch and a really cool movie. Ka-*ching*!

"Mom?"

"Mmm?" my mother answers, fiddling with her turquoise necklace as she gazes at her computer screen. She is not really listening to me. The cozy Thursday-night smell of our meatballs-and-mashed-potatoes dinner hangs in the air, and our stomachs are nice and full, and she's busy with work.

Perfect.

"You know how you're always telling me to make new friends?" I ask softly.

Mom pulls her eyes away from her work and looks at me instead, instantly alert. Mothers everywhere in the animal kingdom are like this with their young, I tell myself nervously. It doesn't mean she's really paying close attention.

"Um–hmm," she says, nodding. "Friends. Well," she corrects me, "I believe I told you not to worry—that you *would* make new friends at Oak Glen. And you have, Emma. Just look at you and Annie Pat! Why, you couldn't have chosen a better friend if you'd ordered her from a catalog." She beams a smile at me.

"And don't forget Kry," I say, sliding in the name—a name that I hope my mom will be hearing a lot in the future. Like this coming Saturday, for instance.

"Cry?" Mom repeats, looking confused.

"Kry Rodriguez, Mom. *You* know. The new girl. She's my friend, too. Our friend, I mean. Mine and Annie Pat's. The three of us are really good friends now."

Liar, liar, pants on fire. But my mom doesn't know that.

And the three of us *will* be friends someday—if it kills me.

Mom blinks, trying to remember when I last talked to her about Kry—which was never, because I was keeping Kry all to myself. "Oh," she finally says. "Well, that's nice, sweetie." Her eyes stray back to the computer screen.

"So anyway," I say, raising my voice a little, "I made this new friend, like you told me to, and I was wondering if I could invite her out to lunch and a movie on Saturday. With you driving. Kry's really nice, Mom."

My mother turns to me, surprised. "But, Emma, you already have plans on Saturday," she says, reminding me. "*Big* plans. Annie Pat and her father are taking you to Marine Universe!"

Mom sometimes forgets what day it is, ever since she started working at home, and she almost always forgets to buy the kind of cereal I like best, and she often forgets to take clothes out of the dryer, and she sometimes forgets to add all the correct ingredients to a recipe. Even cookies! And peanut-butter cookies without the peanut butter are just plain weird.

But she has to remember *this*?

"Marine Universe is off," I inform my mom. "Annie Pat canceled the whole thing," I add, so my mom won't think any of this is my fault.

Big mistake.

"I'm sure you're wrong about that, Emma," Mom says, frowning. "I know how much Annie Pat was looking forward to her special day. She needs to get away from the new baby, even if it's only for a little while."

A toucan's call can be heard up to a half mile away.

And then my mom reaches for the phone.

"No, don't!" I say, squawking the words like a startled toucan.

But it's too late. Mom and Mrs. Masterson are already

talking. "Mmm-hmm, mmm-hmm," my mom murmurs, shooting me a *stay-right-there* glance as I tiptoe toward the door.

It's more of a glare, really, and my heart starts thudding.

"Mmm-hmm," Mom continues. "Oh, for heaven's sake!" She listens to Annie Pat's mother some more. "Well," Mom finally says with a sigh, "I can't tell you how sorry I am, Donna. I don't know what got into Emma, but I intend to find out. *Pronto.*"

Then she makes a few good-bye noises, hangs up the phone, and turns to face me.

And I thought things were bad before!

I have a feeling round three is about to begin.

9

it Seemed Like
a Good idea at the time

It is a cold but sunny Friday morning, and the world smells like wet fallen leaves, and school starts in about twenty minutes, and I have a headache from being yelled at by my mom last night. She told me that not only did I hurt Annie Pat's feelings, which I did by accident, but I lied about what happened, which I did on purpose. (But it seemed like a good idea at the time.)

So I'm not doing *anything* tomorrow—except writing letters of apology to Annie Pat *and* my mom. Ugh. Maybe I should just write a letter of apology to the whole world, while I'm at it!

And now, worst of all, I have to un-invite Kry

Rodriguez to the cool Saturday lunch and movie. We were going to have such a good time that Kry would have wanted to be my friend for sure, even though I'm divorced. Well, not me, but you know what I mean.

And Cynthia would have learned an important lesson. (Not to mess with me.)

"Who are you looking for, the Easter bunny?" EllRay Jakes asks me, teasing. He hops up onto the picnic table the girls usually use, but I don't even tell him to scram—partly because Jared Matthews and Stanley Washington are on their way over to the table, too. And there aren't any other third-grade girls around to help defend it.

"Yeah. Even though it's almost Thanksgiving, I'm looking for bunnies," I say, pretending to be bored. "And here come some now."

"Yo. What's happenin'?" Jared bellows, flinging his grimy, skate-stickered backpack onto the table. Yuck.

"Nothin'," EllRay mumbles, because he's a little

bit scared of Jared, I think. Like I said before, Ell-Ray is the littlest kid in the third grade, and Jared is the biggest. "Emma's just waiting for—"

"I *know* who she's waiting for," Jared interrupts. "Kry Rodriguez, that's who. Her new best friend," he jeers. "Only Cynthia wants her, too."

Even the *boys* know about our battle for Kry? I thought they never noticed anything!

"Who cares what Cynthia wants?" I say—under my breath, of course.

"Ooh!" Stanley says, pretending to be shocked. "I'm gonna tell Cynthia you said that."

"Go ahead and tell," I say, since he'll probably do it anyway. "I'm just trying to be nice to the new girl, that's all."

"Well, now's your chance," Jared says, pointing.

It's true. Kry Rodriguez is heading toward the picnic table! She waves hello at me from across the lawn, then swings her shiny hair back over her shoulders. She is wearing a red fleecy top, black Levis, and black ankle boots.

I really, really, really want a pair of boots like those.

"Hi," I say, jumping off the table so I can meet her halfway—without those nosy boys listening in on every word. "I have to talk to you, Kry. It's important. In fact, I was going to call you last night, only I don't have your phone number yet."

"I wanted to call you, too," Kry says, peeking at me through her long bangs. An *I'm-sorry* look is already spreading across her face. "Because it turns out that we have relatives coming on Saturday. They're staying for a whole week, until after Thanksgiving. So my mom says I can't go out to lunch with you."

I instantly decide that there's no reason to un-invite Kry for Saturday, since she can't come anyway. Why tell her what I almost had to do? "Lunch and a movie," I remind her, because I want Kry to realize just how special Saturday was going to be.

"And a movie," Kry echoes, looking even sadder. "Oh, and by the way," she whispers, "she's divorced, too. My mom, I mean."

Huh?

Hooray!

"Oh. That's too bad," I say with a grown-up-sounding sigh.

Kry shrugs to show me that yeah, it's too bad, but no big deal. She's okay with it. "Where's that girl with the red hair?" she asks, peering around the filling-up lawn area as she changes the subject. "She looks really nice. Maybe you can ask *her* to go with you."

"Her name's Annie Pat. And she *is* nice," I say gloomily. "She used to be my best friend, in fact."

"Used to be?" Kry says, blinking her surprise.

"It's a long story," I tell her as Fiona, Cynthia, and Heather come swooping across the lawn, heading in our direction. They are all dressed in various shades of pink today. Even Cynthia's headband is pink. With sparkles in it.

No sign of Annie Pat yet. I think my headache just got a whole lot worse.

"Kry," Cynthia squeals, giving her a little hug. "You look so cute today. Love your boots!"

"You look cute, too," Kry tells her. "You guys look very—*pink*."

"We are," Cynthia exclaims, as if looking pink is a good thing. She twirls around and then pauses to rearrange her glittering headband. "And next time we dress alike, I'll call you, too, Kry, and tell you what color to wear."

Score—for Cynthia.

"Oh. Thanks, I guess," Kry says weakly. "But I'm not really sure if—"

"It'll be great," Cynthia interrupts, grinning. She shoots me a *ha-ha-on-you* look. "Where's Annie Pat?" she says, hands on her hips.

Does *everyone* have to ask me that?

I suddenly realize that Annie Pat probably isn't even coming to school today. She must have told her mom she had tummy trouble again—and Mrs. Masterson is too worn out from having a new baby to argue with her.

Lucky Annie Pat, to have such a frazzled mom.

"But Cynthia," Heather says in kind of a snotty way, "you'd better not call Annie Pat and Emma the next time we get dressed up, because pink doesn't look good with red hair."

"Everything looks good with red hair," I tell them in a loud, clear voice, and I turn and walk away.

What have I done? I've lost Annie Pat Masterson forever, and she was my very best friend.

I got greedy, that's what happened.

"Hey, Emma," EllRay Jakes calls out from the picnic table. "You forgot your book bag."

"Keep-away," Jared cries, delighted.

"Keep-away!" Stanley chimes in as he tosses my extremely nice book bag to Jared.

Leave it to a bunch of boys to make a bad situation even worse.

10

the Most terrible Saturday in History?

Somehow, I made it through the rest of Friday. It is now Saturday morning, but instead of getting ready to go to Marine Universe with Annie Pat and her dad and no new baby, or getting ready to take Kry Rodriguez out to lunch and a movie, I am sitting alone in my bedroom watching the rain come down. (Outside, of course.)

I do not have a TV in my bedroom, because my mom doesn't approve of TVs in kids' bedrooms. Also, I do not have a computer in my bedroom, because Mom thinks kids should only use the Internet when a grown-up is watching. Watching the actual screen, not the kids.

In my opinion, however, another reason—maybe the real reason—I don't have these things is because extra TVs and computers cost extra money, and extra money is something we do not have ever since my mother started working at home.

Why couldn't she have chosen a new job that pays a lot of money? I will never understand grown-ups—until I am one, and probably not even then.

What I do have in my room is a combination radio and CD player, which my father sent me last Christmas. (He lives in England with his new wife, Annabelle.) But when I am grounded, I am not even allowed to listen to music.

Is my mother the strictest mom in the world? Yes. And is this going to be the most terrible Saturday in history? Probably.

All I'm allowed to do when I'm grounded is read, which doesn't make any sense at all. It's like saying that reading is another part of my punishment, and TV and CDs and the radio are treats.

Really, reading is one of my favorite things in the world—for lots of reasons. For instance, everyone is exactly the same when they read a book. Rich kids, and kids with perfectly straight hair, and undivorced kids read the exact same words that I do. But I get to choose how everyone looks in the book!

Another reason I like reading is that no one can tell me who to like in the book and who to hate. I mean, you can always tell who you're supposed to like, but nobody can make you. You get to decide who's popular—with *you*.

But I don't feel like reading this morning. I prefer to feel a little sorry for myself.

Many hamsters blink only one eye at a time.

I am all alone in the world. Alone except for the person in the condo next door, who is thudding along on his treadmill like a giant hamster. The vibrations shake my bedroom wall.

And alone except for my mom, who keeps coming up with chores for me to do.

"Emma?" Mom calls out from down the hall. "Did you finish writing your apologies?"

"Uh-huh," I say, eyeballing the two letters that practically have sweat marks on them, they were so hard to write.

"And did you gather up all your laundry like I asked you to?"

"Yes," I lie, looking around at the dirty clothes strewn around my room. Because—what's she going to do if I *don't* gather up my laundry? Ground me? Too late!

But then I remember what happened the last time I lied to my mom—about Annie Pat and Marine Universe—and I start gathering. I finish just as Mom steps into my room. "All done," I say, trying not to pant as I stuff the last T-shirt into my laundry basket.

"Good girl. You can help me get the first load started, and then I'd like you to empty all the waste-paper baskets and take the trash out to the Dumpster."

Just like Cinderella! Taking out the trash is my least favorite chore, because other people's garbage smells so yucky. And even though I have to throw our garbage bag up really high to get it over the side of the condo Dumpster, I worry about falling in. Especially today, when it's slippery outside because of the rain.

Mom gives me a challenging look until I mumble, "Okay."

"This is how I spend *every* Saturday," she reminds me.

Never grow up, I remind myself.

⁂ ⁂ ⁂

Mom tells me to take a seat in the kitchen just before lunch. She is holding the apology letter she made me write to her. "We need to talk," she says, looking serious.

Uh-oh. "But why?" I ask her. "Don't you like the letter I wrote? I worked really hard on it."

"It's perfectly fine," she says, giving it an absentminded pat. "Apologies come very easily to you, Emma."

"They do not," I say, trying to keep calm. "I *hate* apologizing—to anyone!"

Mom sighs. "Well," she says, "you obviously know that lying to your mother is wrong, at least."

"Lying to *anyone* is wrong," I tell her, hoping this will give me extra credit.

But Mom doesn't even hear me. "I'm just worried about you lately, sweetie," she says. "You really hurt Annie Pat's feelings, and that's not like you."

It's exactly *like me—when I'm not thinking,* I feel like telling her. *It was a mistake! Can't a per-*

*son make a mistake around here? It's not like you're
so perfect!*

Naturally, I don't say any of this out loud, or
I'd have to sit here forever.

"Didn't it hurt your feelings when Cynthia
stopped being friends with you, Emma?" Mom
asks. "It was only a few weeks ago, after all."

I give a tiny shrug. "I didn't care," I mumble.

"I think you *did* care, honey," my mom says.
"I think you felt really sad and confused when it
happened. And I think that's the way Annie Pat

must have felt when you forgot about her and started going after Kry Rodriguez, just because she's exciting and new."

"But Cynthia shouldn't get to have her," I say, finally daring to argue a little. "Cynthia is mean. That's the whole *point*, Mom. And she gets to have everything!"

"Kry isn't a 'thing,' Emma," my mom says, frowning. "She's a person, and she can make up her own mind about who she wants to be friends with, don't you think?"

"But what if she decides wrong?" I say, trying to make my mom understand.

"Then she'll have made a mistake," Mom says calmly. "And that'll be her problem, Emma. Not yours. Look," she says, leaning forward. "Do you remember when you kept losing your doll clothes after we moved here? And do you remember when you *completely* lost that library book last month, and we had to pay the library fourteen ninety–five to replace it? *Fourteen ninety–five?*

And remember when you lost the front-door key a couple of weeks ago?"

She's gonna bring up *everything*? What do moms do, keep an invisible list?

"I guess," I say reluctantly. "I'm sorry, I'm sorry, I'm sorry."

Mom reaches over to hug me. "Oh, honey, I'm not trying to make you apologize again," she says. "I'm only trying to tell you that being careless with *objects* is one thing. But you can't be careless with people, ever. Especially not the people you care about."

"And I was careless with Annie Pat?" I say, kind of seeing it that way for the first time.

"I think you were," my mom says, nodding.

"Well, you don't have to be mad at me, Mom," I tell her softly. "Because I'm already even madder at myself."

"I am so glad to hear that, Emma," my mom says, hugging me again, only this time there are tears in her eyes.

The weirdest things make her happy—and sad.

"I've got a good idea," she says, changing the subject with food, which always works. "This is a perfect day to bake some pies."

"Pies?" I repeat. "But it's too early to cook for Thanksgiving. They'll get stale, won't they?"

"Not if we eat 'em," Mom says with a grin. "Or give 'em away. Come on, Em—I thought you *liked* pumpkin pie."

Pumpkin pie! "I love it," I say, almost drooling.

"And you didn't get to have any last year, as I recall," my mother continues. "You griped about it for weeks, in fact. And I did the bulk of my holiday shopping yesterday, to beat the crowds, so we have the ingredients. Why *not* make our pies today? And even eat one, if we feel like it!"

"But—but we usually buy pumpkin pie in the store, Mom," I say. "It must be really hard to make." I picture my mother, who really doesn't like to cook, plopping our poor old Halloween pumpkin—which we never got around to carving—into a frozen pie crust and hoping for the best.

"I've actually got a recipe," she says, grinning at me. "And lots of canned pumpkin," she adds. "So let's make our sandwiches and eat them fast, sweetie. We've got some serious pie baking to do!"

γ **11** γ

ReaLLy, ReaLLy,
Very, Very Sorry

Like I told my mom, I hate having to say I'm sorry.
And it's especially hard in person. But it looks like
that's what I'll have to do, because it is Sunday afternoon, and we are on our way over to Annie Pat
Masterson's house so I can give her my apology
letter. Also, we are bringing the Mastersons one
of our pumpkin pies. Also, my mom has a small
present that she has been meaning to take over to
Murphy, the Mastersons' new red-haired baby.

The pumpkin pie looks a little burned on top,
and a chunk of the crust broke off when we got
in the car, but Mom says they'll still appreciate it.
She says that when you have a new baby, you're

desperate for food someone else has made.

Annie Pat, on the other hand, is not desperate. In fact, she will probably slam her bedroom door in my face. And I'll deserve it, too—not because I forgot about going to Marine Universe yesterday, but because I forgot about *her*, my best friend, Annie Pat. At least for a little while.

And that was a wrong thing to do.

"Did Mrs. Masterson say that Annie Pat and her father had a good time at Marine Universe?" I ask gloomily, staring out the car window at the trees whizzing by.

"They didn't go," Mom says, eyes on the road. "Annie Pat was too upset."

"Oh."

That's not good. I start rehearsing my apology all over again.

"What's their house number?" Mom asks, peering out the window at Sycamore Lane, where the Mastersons live.

I've only been to Annie Pat's house once, because

of the baby, but I remember. "Three-fifteen," I mumble, and then *we* are there.

Way too soon.

℀ ℀ ℀

Knock, knock. "Can I come in?" I whisper at Annie Pat's bedroom door, which I happen to know is decorated on the inside with pictures of beautiful jellyfish.

Jellyfish are **95** percent water.

"Nuh-uh," Annie Pat's muffled voice says from behind the door.

"Please?" I say.

No answer. Then, "I'm busy reading about leopard sharks."

I slump down onto the floor outside Annie Pat's room and listen to the grown-ups in the living room cooing over the baby. "Look at those little hands!" Mom marvels, as if she's never seen hands before. *I* have hands, and all she ever notices is whether or not my fingernails are dirty.

Annie Pat's house smells different from ours. Not bad, but different. I knock again, but Annie Pat still doesn't answer. So I slide my apology letter under her door—and listen hard to hear if she tiptoes over to get it.

It is a very good letter, in my opinion, and here is what it says:

Dear Annie Pat,

I am really, really, very, very sorry that I hurt your feelings last week. And do you know what? When I acted bad, it wasn't because I didn't want to be your best friend anymore, and it wasn't because that new girl Kry was so great, even if she does have pretty hair. I just wanted to beat Cynthia, that's all, because she always gets to win. And to decide who should be friends with who. That's just not right.

But I was wrong to forget about you. Will you please forgive me?

I promise never to try to make friends with Kry Rodriguez again. And I promise not to let Cynthia drive me nuts. I was wrong about that, too.

Your sincere friend,
Emma McGraw

Even if I end up with no friends at all—let alone a cool best friend like Annie Pat Masterson, who wants to be a scientist, too—at least I'm doing the right thing.

Annie Pat's door opens a crack, just wide enough for me to see one pigtail and one navy-blue eye. "Say it out loud," she tells me, sounding stern.

"The whole thing? But—but I don't have it memorized," I stammer.

"Just the last part," Annie Pat says.

I wrinkle up my forehead. *Boy,* I think, *she's not making this very easy for me.* "I was wrong," I force myself to say.

"Not that," Annie Pat says from behind the door. "The part after that."

The part after that. I try to remember. "Uh, 'your friend'?" I say, guessing.

Annie Pat's door opens a little more. Now I can see her angry nose. "You were mean to me just the way Cynthia was mean to you, once upon a time," she tells me. "You're exactly like Cynthia, Emma. You dummy."

"I'm *not* like Cynthia," I object—but nicely, and smiling, in spite of her rude remark, so that she won't shut the door again.

I may be a lot of things, but "dummy" isn't one of them. I hope.

"Yes, you are too," Annie Pat insists. "You were trying to decide who would be friends with who, weren't you? And I just knew that pretty soon you were gonna tell everyone, '*Kry Rodriguez is my first-best friend, and Annie Pat*

Masterson is my second-best friend.' Just like Cynthia!"

"I would never say such a dumb thing," I tell Annie Pat. "And like I wrote in the letter, I promise I won't try to make friends with Kry Rodriguez anymore. I'll forget she's even in our class."

"I don't care about that, Emma," Annie Pat says, opening her bedroom door even more. Tears make her eyes look even bigger than usual, and that's saying something. "I mean, I like Kry Rodriguez, too," she says. "Who wouldn't? I just don't want you to forget about being friends with me, that's all."

"Never," I say, crossing my heart and hoping to die.

(Not really, but you know what I mean.)

"Then you may enter," Annie Pat says, sounding like a queen.

"Thank you for forgiving me," I tell her humbly.

And I really, really mean it.

turkeys drool,
Best friends Rule!

"Hey, Kry, what is your family going to do to-morrow?" Cynthia asks Kry Rodriguez at lunch on Wednesday, the day before Thanksgiving. Most of the girls in our class have gathered at the picnic table because it's so pretty outside. The sun is shining, and orange and gold leaves are blowing all around the nearby playground like little holiday decorations, and two scrub jays squawk like crazy in the branches above our heads.

Cynthia plays with a tiny plastic turkey that is pinned to her pure white sweatshirt as she waits for Kry to answer. I wonder where she got it? I wouldn't mind having one.

Kry swallows a bite of her pita-bread sandwich and takes a sip of milk. "We have relatives staying," she finally says above the uproar—as loud as a garbage truck—the boys are making at a nearby table, and then she smiles at me, because I already know about the relatives.

Cynthia does not like that smile, but I don't even care enough to think, *Score!* Whoever Kry wants to be friends with is just fine.

(Of course, if she wants to hang out with Annie Pat and me, that would be really, really, very, very fine. And Annie Pat agrees with me!)

"We're going to my grandma's house in San Diego," Heather reports, unasked. The long skinny braid that usually falls across her face has a little plastic turkey on its elastic band that matches Cynthia's, I notice.

"And my family is flying to Seattle," Fiona says, looking important.

And there's a third little turkey, pinned to the sleeve of Fiona's shirt.

Matching turkeys! I change my mind about wanting one of those pins.

"Lucky you, Fiona," Annie Pat says, looking jealous. She has never been on an airplane. Neither have I, for that matter, but I'm supposed to fly to England next summer to visit my dad, and that ought to count for about a hundred trips.

"We *love* Thanksgiving," one of the church-friends says happily.

"Us, too," one of the neighbor-friends says. "Pumpkin pie with whipped cream on top!"

Annie Pat and I exchange green and groany looks at the very mention of pumpkin pie, because last Sunday, we ate more than our share—for this year *and* for next year. When we are hungry for pumpkin pie again, we'll be ten years old.

Double digits!

"And Thanksgiving is fun 'cause there are always lots of little cousins to play with," Kry chimes in. It's more like she's a normal part of our class, now, and no one is trying too hard to impress her anymore.

(Well, except for some of the boys, but that's another story.)

"What are you and your mom doing for Thanksgiving, Emma?" Kry asks.

I grin and slide a happy look in Annie Pat's direction. "We got invited to eat over at Annie Pat's house," I tell her—and everyone. "We're bringing the stuffing!"

Because the right stuffing is nearly as important as pumpkin pie. And other people's stuffing is just plain weird.

"We're gonna have fu-u-u-un," Annie Pat says. "I like to put black olives on all my fingers and then eat 'em!"

Poor Annie Pat had been thinking that she and Murphy would be the only kids at their holiday meal. And you can't really count on babies for a good time.

"What about you, Cynthia?" one of the neighbor-friends asks. "What are you gonna do tomorrow?"

"Same old, same old," Cynthia says, smoothing back her already-smooth hair while she pretends to be grown-up and bored—about a *major holiday.*

And that's just rude! Also, it's probably unpatriotic.

"But me and my mom always go clothes shopping the day *after* Thanksgiving," Cynthia adds, "and that's fun. We get up real early, when it's still dark outside."

"Oooh, shopping," Fiona and Heather echo, as if that's really the best part about Thanksgiving. Talk about missing the point!

Annie Pat and I barely look at each other before we start to giggle, and then to laugh, because we just can't help it. And then Kry Rodriguez starts laughing, too. *"Turkeys drool, best friends rule!"* I whisper to the two of them, which just gets all three of us laughing more.

Where did *that* goofy saying come from? Maybe I made it up! But, speaking as a future nature scientist, I do not think turkeys really can drool.

Only male turkeys gobble.

And it would be kind of yucky if they could.

"*What* did you say?" Cynthia asks, springing to her feet. "Were you guys whispering bad things about me?"

"Course not," Kry says, soothing Cynthia's ruffled feathers. And she's not lying, either, because Kry didn't necessarily know who I was talking about when I said "turkeys."

"Well okay, then," Cynthia says with a sniff.

"Sit down, Cynthia," Heather coos, patting the picnic bench next to her.

"Have some raisins," Fiona says, rattling her little red cardboard box in a tempting way.

Things are quiet again at our lunch table—in

comparison to the boys' table, anyway.

And I think how happy I am, even though I'm divorced. I'm happy to have a best friend like Annie Pat Masterson, who I will be visiting Marine Universe with the Saturday after Thanksgiving, and a maybe-new-friend like Kry Rodriguez, and even to have an ex-friend like Cynthia Harbison, who I'm not even mad at anymore, for some reason.

I have that . . . that *full* feeling you get when things with you and your friends are just right.

I guess you could say I'm feeling thankful.

A whole day early, too!